Willie and Shadow
A dog and a cat

M. Balm
A librarian

Dr. Izzy Dedyet
A doctor

Kate Klise

43 Old Cemetery Road: Book Four

The Phantom of the Post Office

Illustrated by **M. Sarah Klise**

Harcourt

Houghton Mifflin Harcourt
BOSTON   NEW YORK   2012

URGENT

Text copyright © 2012 by Kate Klise
Illustrations copyright © 2012 by M. Sarah Klise

Harcourt Children's Books is an imprint of
Houghton Mifflin Harcourt Publishing Company.

www.hmhbooks.com

Library of Congress Cataloging-in-Publication Data
Klise, Kate.
The phantom of the post office / Kate Klise; illustrated by M. Sarah Klise.
p. cm.
(43 Old Cemetery Road : bk. 4)   [1. Letters—Fiction. 2. Postal service—Fiction.
3. Technology—Fiction. 4. Ghosts—Fiction. 5. Haunted houses—Fiction.
6. Humorous stories.] I. Klise, M. Sarah, ill. II. Title.
PZ7.K684Ph 2012
[Fic]—dc23   2011027316

ISBN 978-0-547-51974-6

Designed by M. Sarah Klise

Manufactured in the United States of America
DOC 10 9 8 7 6 5 4 3 2 1
4500348169

4860 4572 5/12

CONFIDENTIAL

As long as there are postmen, life will have zest.
William James

Welcome to Spence Mansion,

a haunted house occupied by

Ignatius B. Grumply
A writer
DAD

Olive C. Spence
A ghost writer
MOM

Seymour Hope
A young artist
SON

To our knowledge, this is the only family in
America that does not own

a telephone   a television   or a single
                                            gaming device.

But if you're feeling sorry
for this family, **don't.**

Because the occupants of Spence Mansion have been busy
with more important matters,
                            such as creating
                            a bestselling book titled

**43
Old
Cemetery
Road**

which they publish three
chapters at a time

and send to readers by
old-fashioned mail.

This requires many trips to the local
post office . . .

and many trips to their mailbox, which is filled
most days with fan mail from all over the world.

But one day
not long ago
this family
received
a most unusual
letter
from a most
unusual fan.

And that is where our
story begins.

P.O. BOX 5
GHASTLY, ILLINOIS

POSTMORTEM

OCCUPANTS
43 OLD CEMETERY ROAD
GHASTLY, ILLINOIS

```
              P.O. BOX 5
          GHASTLY, ILLINOIS


JANUARY 23


DEAR OLIVE, IGNATIUS, AND SEYMOUR:

THE END IS NEAR. BEWARE!

YOURS TRULY,

A FAN
```

43 Old Cemetery Road
Third Floor
Ghastly, Illinois

January 24

Dear Olive and Iggy,

Did you see the fan letter we received today? It's a bit creepy.

If we had a phone, we could call the sheriff. Isn't it time we got a phone? I'm tired of writing letters.

Love,

        —Seymour

O.C.S.

Ghost Writer in Residence
43 Old Cemetery Road, The Cupola
Ghastly, Illinois

January 24

Dear Seymour,

Tired of writing letters? Bite your tongue, young man. The day you're tired of writing letters is the day you're tired of living.

I never had a telephone during my life. I don't intend to have one in my afterlife, either. Besides, I think the sheriff has far better things to do than track down the person who wrote that silly letter. Beware, my foot! What kind of fan would try to frighten us with such nonsense?

Just ignore the letter, dear. We have more pressing matters to discuss, such as our book. We've promised our readers three new chapters by March 1. All the more reason *not* to have a telephone.

Yours in the written word,

Olive

IGNATIUS B. GRUMPLY

A WRITER IN RESIDENCE

43 OLD CEMETERY ROAD   2ND FLOOR   GHASTLY, ILLINOIS

January 25

Seymour Hope
Third floor
43 Old Cemetery Road
Ghastly, Illinois

Dear Seymour,

I know you've wanted a phone for a while now. And just between you and me, I thi

I think there is nothing more disagreeable than modern technology.

Olive! I wish you wouldn't read over my shoulder.

I'm sorry, dear. But have you seen children these days with those tiny electronic contraptions they stare at from morning till night? They look like ninnies!

I suspected you'd have strong opinions about this.

Oh, Iggy. You agree with me, don't you?

I do. But I also know how hard it is to be an only child. Like Seymour, I grew up without brothers or sisters. Seymour has terrific pets. He adores Willie and Shadow and the new kittens, but the boy needs *human* friends. And I hate to tell you this, Olive, but the way young people make friends now is with their phones and computers.

Phooey. I don't buy it.

Or do you mean you don't *like* it?

That, too. I don't believe that meeting someone on the telephone or computer is the way to establish a true friendship. Isn't it much more fun to write letters?

Maybe to your generation, but not to children today.

Then we must convince them of it. Oh, Iggy, I just had the most brilliant notion!

I'm listening.

We shall write the next three chapters of our book about friendship—the *real* kind of friendship you make through letters.

I like it. And I bet Seymour will, too.

Of course he will. It's a wonderful idea!

And maybe it will help him forget about that strange fan letter. You're really not concerned about it, Olive?

Heavens, no. Just ignore it, Iggy.

If you say so. Now the only thing we have to figure out is how to deliver our new chapters to readers when the post office closes its doors for good.

Don't be absurd. The post office can't close. How would people communicate without letters?

Take a look at today's paper.

THE GHASTLY TIMES

Sunday, January 25
Cliff Hanger, Editor

"We're Living in Ghastly Times"

$1.50
Morning Edition

Ghastly Post Office to Close
Regular mail will be replaced by VEXT-mail on March 1

Sadder than a dead letter. More baffling than an illegible address.

That's how Sue Perstishus described the news that the Ghastly Post Office will close for good on February 28.

"I just never thought it would come to this," said Perstishus, Ghastly's postmaster and only mail carrier.

Founded in 1837, the Ghastly Post Office has a long and colorful history.

"In the old days the postmaster delivered everyone's mail by horse and buggy," said Perstishus.

But just as people have found faster ways to travel, so too have they found more efficient ways to communicate. In recent years faxes, e-mail and text messages have greatly reduced the volume of mail delivered by the U.S. Postal Service.

Now a new technology called VEXT-mail is expected to replace all forms of written communication. VEXT-mail is a video-enhanced text messaging system made possible by a wireless electronic veil worn on the head of the user.

"I have no idea how it works," said Perstishus with a shudder. "New technology makes me nervous."

VEXT-mail was unveiled last week by Sal U. Tayshuns, the new U.S. postmaster general.

Sue Perstishus is saddened by the news.

"I've chosen Ghastly as our first VEXT-mail town," said Tayshuns at a press conference in Washington, D.C. "Ghastly is a small town in middle America. It's the perfect place to test this new and exciting technology. I just know the folks there will love it!"

The Ghastly Post Office will close on February 28 and reopen as a VEXT-mail center on March 1.

Flu Season Is Here

It's that time of year again, folks. Time for bugs, viruses and various forms of creeping crud that most of us simply call the flu.

Experts say people can avoid the flu by taking simple precautions.

"I recommend flu vaccines for most of my patients and hand washing for all of them," said Dr. Izzy Dedyet.

Dedyet suggests washing hands with soap and water for at least 20 seconds. "That's long enough to sing 'Happy Birthday' twice," said Dedyet. He also teaches patients to cough and sneeze into their sleeves rather than hands to decrease

(Continued on page 2, column 1)

FLU *(Continued from page 1, column 2)*

Dr. Izzy Dedyet says frequent hand washing is important.

the likelihood of spreading illness.

Dedyet acknowledged that doctors are never certain what strain the influenza virus will take from year to year. "All we really know is that flu activity usually peaks in the U.S. in January or February," he said.

Order Now Don't miss the new chapters!

43 Old Cemetery Road

Wynonna Fye to Visit for One Month

What do you do with an 11-year-old girl from Minneapolis who's addicted to digital devices?

Send her to live for a month with her favorite uncle, M. Balm.

"My niece is a good girl with a bad habit," said Balm, chief librarian at the Ghastly Public Library. "She thinks she can't live without her high-tech gadgets."

According to Balm, Wynonna "Wy" Fye talks and texts on her phone day and night. Balm said he's not opposed to cell phones. "I have one myself," he stated. "They can be useful in times of emergency. I just don't like to see people turned into zombies by their digital gizmos."

Balm said he's eager to help his niece kick her cell phone dependency. "I plan to prove to Wy that she can live for one month without using a cell phone."

How?

Librarian has low-tech plans for high-tech niece.

"By betting her that she can't!" said Balm, beaming.

Wy Fye is scheduled to arrive on Saturday. She will spend the entire month of February in Ghastly.

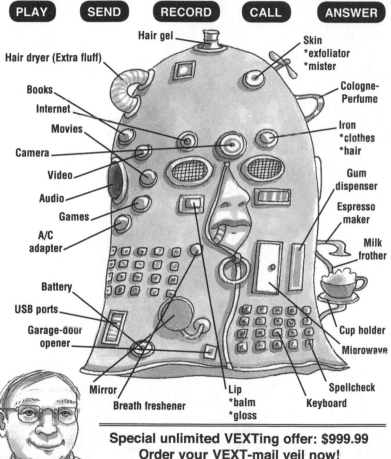

January 26

Wynonna Fye
300 Nicollet Mall
Minneapolis, MN 55401

Dear Wynonna,

It would take me an hour to tap out a response to your text message on my cell phone, so I shall reply the old-fashioned way—by letter.

I think you'll be pleasantly surprised by all Ghastly has to offer. Did you know it's haunted? That's right. The ghost of Olive C. Spence lives here. But don't worry. Olive is a delight. Let me tell you a little bit about her.

Olive was born and raised in Ghastly. She grew up on Old Cemetery Road, where she loved reading mysteries and scary books. She dreamed of becoming a published author and even built a $32\frac{1}{2}$-room mansion on her family's old property so that she would have the perfect place to write. She called the house Spence Mansion. That's where she held elaborate parties to celebrate the completion of her manuscripts.

Sadly, instead of becoming a bestselling author, Olive became famous for receiving more rejection letters than any writer in history. Some publishers sent her manuscripts back with a single word stamped across the top—REJECTED.

Well, as you can imagine, failure took its toll. In her final years, Olive, who never married or had children, rarely left her mansion. When she died in 1911 at the age of 93, the cause of death was listed as "a heart broken by the continued rejection by publishers."

Depressed? Don't be. Because this is where the story starts getting interesting. Shortly before her death, Olive made a solemn vow to haunt her house and the town of Ghastly for eternity—or until one of her mysteries was published. And haunt it she did. From stealing muffins at the local diner to tormenting renters who dared to live in her house, Olive made her presence known.

Enter Ignatius B. Grumply, a down-on-his-luck writer who rented Spence Mansion last summer. Believe me when I tell you it was not love at first sight between Olive and Ignatius. Far from it. Olive teased Ignatius mercilessly in the beginning. (She even dropped a chandelier on his head one night!) But in time, the two became friends and writing partners. Last fall they adopted a young boy named Seymour Hope who had been abandoned by his parents.

And now the trio—Olive, Ignatius, and Seymour—lives together at Spence Mansion, where Olive and Ignatius are cowriting a book called *43 Old Cemetery Road*. Seymour is the illustrator. He's a very sweet boy. I think you'll like him a lot, and I know you'll love their book. It's a bestseller! So you see, there's a happy ending to this story. Olive C. Spence, who died feeling like a failure, has become the world's most successful ghost writer.

Well, that's a long way of saying pack comfortable reading clothes. I plan to introduce you to some good books while you're in Ghastly, which I hope you'll find anything but boring.

See you soon!

Love,

Uncle M.

P.O. BOX 5
GHASTLY, ILLINOIS

POSTMORTEM

OCCUPANTS
43 OLD CEMETERY ROAD
GHASTLY, ILLINOIS

P.O. BOX 5
GHASTLY, ILLINOIS

JANUARY 27

DEAR OLIVE, IGNATIUS, AND SEYMOUR:

DON'T YOU SEE? WE ARE A DYING BREED.

DO SOMETHING . . . BEFORE IT'S TOO
LATE.

YOURS TRULY,

A FAN

43 Old Cemetery Road
Third Floor
Ghastly, Illinois

January 28

Ms. Sue Perstishus
Postmaster, Ghastly Post Office
2 Dead Letter Drive
Ghastly, Illinois

Dear Ms. Perstishus,

We've been getting some strange fan mail from post office box 5. Can you tell me who lives at that house? The letters are stamped POSTMORTEM, whatever that means.

Thanks for your help!

　　—Seymour Hope

P.S. I'm sorry the post office is closing, but I'm excited about VEXT-mail. It sounds super cool.

Sue Perstishus

Postmaster, Ghastly Post Office

2 Dead Letter Drive   Ghastly, Illinois

January 29

Seymour Hope
43 Old Cemetery Road
Third floor
Ghastly, Illinois

Dear Seymour,

Post office box 5 is not the address of a house.
Rather, it's an actual box here at the Ghastly Post
Office.

You might not know this because your mail is delivered to the mailbox at Spence Mansion's side door.
But some people prefer to receive their mail in private
boxes here at the post office.

I'm no artist,
but here's
my sketch
of post office
box 5.
You can
see what
it looks like.

Now, after all that, I'm sorry that I'm not allowed to tell you who has the key to this box. When I became post-master of Ghastly, I took an oath to protect the privacy of all my patrons, including those who send letters *post-mortem*. (That's Latin for "after death.")

I wish I had time to write more, but I have to get ready for my first VEXT-mail meeting with Mr. Tayshuns, the new postmaster general and my boss. I hope I can figure out how to work this VEXT-mail veil. (I know you kids like all this new technology, but I can't stand it!)

Sincerely,

Sue Perstishus

Sue Perstishus

Sal U. Tayshuns: This is Sal U. Tayshuns sending a VEXT-mail message to Sue Perstishus. Sue, are you there? I can't see you. Can you see me?

Sue Perstishus: Yes, Mr. Tayshuns. I can see you fine. Can you see me?

Sal U. Tayshuns: No, I can't. Adjust your veil. It should fit snugly over your head.

Sue Perstishus: Um, okay. Can you see me now?

Sal U. Tayshuns: No, I still can't see you.

Sue Perstishus: Uh-oh. Now I can't see you, either. Probably because I have this VEXT-mail veil covering my eyes.

Sal U. Tayshuns: Hmm. It appears there are some hiccups to be worked out with this technology. Can you at least hear me?

Sue Perstishus: Sort of. The connection's not great.

Sal U. Tayshuns: Well, I'm glad you just ate. But if you can't hear me, Sue, just read the text scrolling above your eyes. VEXT-mail provides a written record of everything said within 5 yards of the veil. We can print out a transcript whenever we like.

Sue Perstishus: It's too dark under this veil to read anything, sir. But it sounds like that might come in handy.

Sal U. Tayshuns: Andy? Who's Andy? Never mind, Sue. I have good news and bad news.

Sue Perstishus: I'm losing my job, aren't I?

Sal U. Tayshuns: I'm afraid so. We won't need a postmaster in Ghastly once we transition to VEXT-mail. But here's the good news: There'll be an opening for a VEXTmaster. All you have to do is learn the new technology.

Sue Perstishus: I'm not very good at that sort of thing.

Sal U. Tayshuns: It's a cinch, Sue. And once you get the hang of it, you'll love using VEXT-mail.

Sue Perstishus: I suppose I could try.

Sal U. Tayshuns: That's the spirit! Now, there's one other thing. You'll need to get the keys back from everyone in Ghastly who has a post office box.

Sue Perstishus: Er. Um.

Sal U. Tayshuns: Did you just call me dumb?

Sue Perstishus: No, sir. I said "um."

Sal U. Tayshuns: I don't appreciate being called dumb.

Sue Perstishus: Sir, I'm afraid you're not hearing me. These veils are a little unreliable. I simply said—

Sal U. Tayshuns: You wish I were *dead?* That is no way to speak to the new postmaster general. I'm going to ignore these remarks and ask that you . . . Now what are you doing? Turn your veil toward magnetic north. Oh, forget it. Just get the keys from everyone in Ghastly who has a post office box. Huh? What? I can't hear a word you're saying, Sue. Never mind. I'll VEXT you later.

P.O. BOX 5
GHASTLY, ILLINOIS

POSTMORTEM

OCCUPANTS
43 OLD CEMETERY ROAD
GHASTLY, ILLINOIS

```
                P.O. BOX 5
           GHASTLY, ILLINOIS


JANUARY 30


DEAR OLIVE, IGNATIUS, AND SEYMOUR:

IF YOU DON'T ACT QUICKLY, THERE
WILL BE A CURSE UPON YOUR HOUSE.

YOURS TRULY,

A FAN
```

43 Old Cemetery Road
Third Floor
Ghastly, Illinois

January 31

Dear Olive,

I just opened today's mail. We received another weird fan letter. Don't you think we should

Ignore it, dear. It's obviously a prank from someone with too much time on his or her hands. Besides, we have business to discuss. With the post office closing, we need to find a new way to deliver our serialized novel to readers. I'm thinking carrier pigeons might be the answer.

Olive, I know just how we'll send our new chapters—by VEXT—mail. It's going to be the coolest thing ever! With VEXT—mail, people will be able to read our stories while they ride bikes or swim or drive.

Good heavens. We're not doing anything of the kind.

Why not?

Because we're making a book, dear.

But Olive, with VEXT—mail it doesn't have to be just a book. It can have games and music and videos with 3-D effects.

I consider such things not only unnecessary, but vaguely offensive.

What do you mean?

Seymour, darling, you might find this hard to believe, but one day you'll want to spend some private time with a girl you fancy. And when you do, you'll want to read to her from a plain old book.

That's disgusting. I don't want to do that!

Not today. But maybe when you're a bit older.

When I'm older, there aren't going to be books. There'll be VEXT—mail veils. And if I'm with a girl, we'll each have our own veil so we can watch movies or read books or play games or whatever—separately. There's even a button for hair gel. Oh, and there's a gum dispenser, too!

What you're describing is the definition of vulgar.

Oh, Olive. You're just old-fashioned.

Yes, I am. I'm also your mother now. And I make the rules.

Every kid except me has a cell phone, video games, and a flat-screen.

We have some lovely flat screens in the parlor—several depicting me, in fact.

Olive, those flat screens are <u>oil paintings</u>. I'm talking about a screen for playing video games.

Video games? No, no, no. I've heard about those horrible things and I get a sick headache just thinking about them. Now wipe that pout off your face.

I'm not pouting.

Then stop holding your breath. You're beet red.

I feel hot. Do I have a fever?

I highly doubt it. You've just worked yourself up into a frenzy over this VEXT-mail nonsense. Take a deep breath and think a pleasant thought.

All right. I'll try.

That's my Seymour. Wait. What are you doing now? Darling, you suddenly look very pale. Oh, no! We'd better get you ... Good heavens! Your knees are buckling. Seymour, have you ... fainted?

Greater Ghastly Memorial Hospital

4 Morgue Way
Ghastly, Illinois

Patient name: _____ SEYMOUR HOPE _____

Date of admission: _____ JANUARY 31 _____

Symptoms: _____ CHILLS, FEVER, DIZZINESS _____

Admitted by: _____ IZZY DEDYET, MD _____

Diagnosis: _____ PHANTOM FLU _____

Recommended treatment: _____ BED REST, FLUIDS _____

_____

THE GHASTLY TIMES

Sunday, February 1

Cliff Hanger, Editor

"We're Living in Ghastly Times"

$1.50

Morning Edition

Phantom Flu Strikes Ghastly

A strange virus has arrived in Ghastly that creeps up on victims suddenly, causing them to develop high fevers before turning pale and fainting.

"I've never seen anything like it," said Dr. Izzy Dedyet, "I'm calling it the phantom flu because it's strange, mysterious and downright scary."

Last night Dedyet admitted Seymour Hope to Greater Ghastly Memorial Hospital. "He's too contagious for visitors," said Dr. Dedyet. "I don't even want him sending letters home for fear he could spread the virus by mail. The best thing Seymour can do is rest in peace, especially after that harrowing trip to the hospital."

Hope is too contagious for visitors.

Hope arrived at the hospital in a car driven by his father, Ignatius B. Grumply. The phoneless family was unable to call for an ambulance.

Wy Asks Why

Wynonna "Wy" Fye arrived in Ghastly yesterday afternoon, where she was greeted by her uncle, M. Balm, and a stack of library books.

"I told Wy to choose a scary book to read while she's staying with me," said Balm, chief librarian at the Ghastly Public Library. "When Wy asked why, I told her there's nothing like a scary book to help a person forget just about anything, even her beloved cell phone."

Fye, age 11, chose *The Phantom of the Opera* by Gaston Leroux. "It's a classic thriller about a phantom who haunts box seat number 5 in the Paris Opera House," said Balm. "I think it's a great choice!"

M. Balm has made a bet with his niece. "If Wy can refrain from talking, texting, tweeting or playing games on a cell phone

Fye will try to spend one month without using a cell phone.

for the entire month of February, I will return her phone when she leaves Ghastly on March 1."

"OMG," said Fye, rolling her eyes. "Thank goodness February is the shortest month. It's not a leap year, is it?"

(No, it's not. February has just 28 days this year.)

Postmaster Vexed by VEXT-mail
"I'm nervous about this new service," says Perstishus

Some will call it a cell phone. Others will call it a microcomputer and mobile gaming device. Still others will call it a personal cappuccino maker, home theater and hair salon—all in one.

But Ghastly Postmaster Sue Perstishus has another way to describe the new VEXT-mail veil: *nerve-racking.*

"It took me half an hour to figure out how to turn the darn thing on," said Perstishus. "And even then, I could barely hear or see a thing."

Perstishus recently tested the soon-to-be-released device. In addition to confessing her technical frustrations, Perstishus said she's uneasy about the transition from old-fashioned mail to VEXT-mail.

"I don't think Mr. Tayshuns understands what this could mean for our town and its safety," said Perstishus, who is known for having a nervous streak. "We all know this town is haunted by the ghost of Olive C. Spence. But do you think she's the

Ghastly postmaster struggles with VEXT-mail veil.

only one? Have you never felt the presence of someone else?"

When asked to name names, Perstishus said simply, "I cannot. I will say only that I'm nervous about this new service."

Remember to wash your hands vigorously during flu season and every season.

Greater Ghastly Memorial Hospital

O.C.S.

Ghost Writer in Residence
43 Old Cemetery Road, The Cupola
Ghastly, Illinois

February 1

Dear Iggy,

Your reckless driving last night could've killed Seymour. Imagine driving 100 miles per hour, rippity snort, to the hospital. I almost fell off the bumper!

In the future, will you *please* be more careful? And wash your hands, dear. I don't want you to catch the flu, too. Influenza can be deadly, especially for older people.

Love,

Olive

IGNATIUS B. GRUMPLY
A WRITER IN RESIDENCE

February 1

Olive C. Spence
The Cupola
43 Old Cemetery Road
Ghastly, Illinois

Dear Olive,

You rode with us to the hospital? I should've kno

Of course I rode with you! I had to make sure
Seymour was in good hands. And now I'm sure.
Dr. Dedyet is a very smart man.

Yes, he is. And our son is a very smart boy. I'm
beginning to think Seymour is right about the
wisdom of having a phone at Spence Mansion. We
could've called an ambulance last night.

Fiddlesticks! You know I loathe modern technology.
Besides, I thought we agreed that we needed to teach
children, including Seymour, about the joys of letter
writing. We were going to write the next three

chapters of our book about friendships born through letters, remember?

I do. Unfortunately, I know little about the matter, Olive. You're the only friend I've ever made through letters.

Oh, dear. Well, I suppose I shall have to write this next installment alone. Wait! I just had the most glorious idea.

Yes?

I shall dig up my old letters from my best friend from childhood. Do you think readers would enjoy mulling over our correspondence?

I know I would. You've never mentioned your best friend before. Who was she?

He, dear. His name was Weston Peece.

Oh.

And he was a *prince* of a man. I'm sure I have his old letters around here somewhere.

I'll help you look for them.

I have a better idea. Why don't you pop over to the hospital and deliver the soup I made to Seymour?

We're not allowed to visit, remember? Dr. Dedyet said absolutely no visitors.

You're right. But couldn't you devise a clever delivery system, perhaps with a tray on a rope tied to his hospital window? You'll think of something, dear, while I dig out my old letters from Weston. I can't wait to reread them. I know just where they are.

Is this Weston guy still alive?

Heavens, no. We were the same age. He must've died decades ago.

And you don't see him . . . around?

No. I guess he didn't have any unfinished business.

Good.

Iggy! You're not jealous, are you?

I think "relieved" is the word. But don't mind me. I've got a sick tray to rig up.

Seymour,

I'm going to write the next
installment of our book about
my dear old friend Weston
Peece. I hope you enjoy reading
about him!

Love,

Olive

43 Old Cemetery Road

How can I possibly describe my best friend,
Weston? How can I describe a friendship that lasted
86 years?

I shall start at the beginning because beginnings are important in books, as well as in life. And
how do the best friendships begin—with a glance?
A word? A smile?

My friendship with Weston began with a letter he wrote and delivered to my front door.

May 17, 1825

Dear Olive C. Spence,

My name is Weston Peece. I am 7 years old. My family just moved to Ghastly. I hear you are 7 years old, too. Do you want to be friends? I've never had a friend before, but I would like to have one.

I know how to read. If you want, we could meet under that big apple tree next to your house, and I could read you a good book.

Yours truly,
Weston Peece

Of course, I knew how to read, too. But I accepted Weston's invitation. We met under my apple tree the following afternoon and spent hours reading aloud to each other. We became best friends that day and remained so until the day I died.

February 2

Seymour Hope
Patient, Greater Ghastly Memorial Hospital
4 Morgue Way
Ghastly, Illinois

Dear Seymour,

I'm so sorry to hear you're sick. I was hoping to introduce
you to my niece while she's in town. She's such a dear girl,
but I worry about her.

When Wynonna was little, she always had a smile on her
face and a kind word to say to everyone. Now she sulks and
pouts. If she's smiled once since her arrival, I haven't seen it.

Maybe it's just a phase she's going through, but I blame her
cell phone. In the past year I'll bet Wynonna has sent more
than ten thousand text messages to her so-called friends. But
I fear she has very few *real* friends.

I had hoped that by introducing her to you, I could help
Wynonna learn how to make and be a friend again. Now
that you're in the hospital, that job has fallen to me. And
dare I admit how tempted I am to simply give her *back* her
blasted phone so she'll stop pestering me for it?

Fortunately, I know the perfect person I can lend Wynonna's cell phone to: your father. Ignatius can use it to call you while you're in the hospital. I'll be happy to get rid of the thing so that I don't have to keep hiding it from Wynonna.

Poor girl. I'm looking at her right now, fidgeting on the sofa in the children's section, trying to read *The Phantom of the Opera*. She was a voracious reader when she was younger. But once again, I blame her cell phone addiction for her inability to focus.

Now she's shivering. Maybe I need to turn up the heat in the library. Except, wait—now she's sweating. Well, that's odd. Her eyes are rolling back and . . . Oh no! She just fell off the sofa! I must call an ambulance.

Yours posthaste,

M.BalM

M. Balm

P.S. Don't worry. I'll drop off the cell phone to your father, as promised.

Greater Ghastly Memorial Hospital
4 Morgue Way
Ghastly, Illinois

Patient name: _____WYNONNA FYE_____

Date of admission: _____FEBRUARY 2_____

Symptoms: _____CHILLS, FEVER, DIZZINESS_____

Admitted by: _____IZZY DEDYET, MD_____

Diagnosis: _____PHANTOM FLU_____

Recommended treatment: _____BED REST, FLUIDS_____

_____

SPECIAL NOTE: PATIENT'S UNCLE HAS REQUESTED THAT ALL DIGITAL TEMPTATIONS BE REMOVED FROM HER ROOM.

Date: _February 3_

To: _Wynonna Fye_
    Room 12

Dear Wynonna,

Welcome to Ghastly. Nothing like the flu to make you feel right at home, eh?

I'd stop by to say hello, but Dr. Dedyet won't let me leave my bed. He did agree to deliver this note to you, though. Let me know if you get it.

Yours with a fever and the chills,

   —Seymour Hope

P.S. In case you're wondering, this is what I look like.

P.P.S. I'm in room 5, if you want to write back. Ask Dr. Dedyet to deliver the note for you.

Date: February 4

To: Seymour Hope
Room 5

Dear Seymour,

Got it! And yeah, I know. Nothing like the flu.

Hey, do u have a cell phone I can borrow? My uncle wants me 2 read <u>The Phantom of the Opera</u>. But OMG, it's like 300 pages. ☹ I want 2 C if any of my peeps @ home have read it and can tell me what it's about.

So LMK if u have a c/phone, k?

TTYL.

Wynonna Fye
(but you can call me Wy)
Room 12

P.S. Your drawing made me LOL. Here's what I look like.

Date: February 4

To: Wynonna Fye
    Room 12

Hi, Wy.

Sorry. No cell here—and I've never read that book.

But if you want, I could read it and tell you what it's about. I like stories about phantoms and ghosts. ☺

        —Seymour

P.S. Loved your pic, but what does TTYL mean? And LMK? And LOL? And OMG?

Date: February 5

To: Seymour Hope
Room 5

Dear Seymour,

Oh my gosh (OMG), I'm laughing out loud (LOL) at your note. Let me know (LMK) what you think of this novel and I'll talk to you later (TTYL).

WY

P.S. Here's the book!

Don't miss

The *Phantom* of the *Opera*

Everyone thinks the phantom is only
a superstition until . . .

**BEST
SELLER!**

Gaston Leroux

P.O. BOX 5
GHASTLY, ILLINOIS

GHASTLY
AM
FEB 5
·IL·

POSTMORTEM

OCCUPANTS
43 OLD CEMETERY ROAD
GHASTLY, ILLINOIS

P.O. BOX 5
GHASTLY, ILLINOIS

FEBRUARY 5

DEAR OLIVE AND IGNATIUS:

NOW DO YOU BELIEVE ME? DO
SOMETHING . . . BEFORE IT'S
TOO LATE.

IF YOU DON'T, I SHALL STEAL
A LETTER ONE NIGHT SOON AT
THE STROKE OF MIDNIGHT.

YOURS TRULY,

A FAN

IGNATIUS B. GRUMPLY

A WRITER IN RESIDENCE

43 OLD CEMETERY ROAD **2ND FLOOR** **GHASTLY, ILLINOIS**

February 6

Seymour Hope
Patient, Greater Ghastly Memorial Hospital
4 Morgue Way
Ghastly, Illinois

Dear Seymour,

I've spent several maddening days trying to figure
out how to turn on the cell phone M. Balm lent me.
I wanted to call and hear how you're feeling, but until
I learn how to work this contraption, I'll have to

Is that a telephone?

Olive, you startled me.

*Answer my question, Iggy. Is that or is that not a
telephone?*

It is. I wanted to call Seymour. I checked with Dr.
Dedyet and he said it's perfectly fine if I call.

On that thing?

It's a cell phone, Olive. They're quite small.

I don't like the looks of it. How does it work?

I'm not sure. We need Seymour to teach us.

Or we could rely instead on good old-fashioned letters.

Yes, I suppose we could. Speaking of letters, what do you think of our latest fan letter?

I don't think about it at all. Why should I?

That threat about stealing a letter at midnight? It's a bit odd. I wonder if we should ask Sue Perstishus. I know she's busy, but

Of course Sue's busy! She doesn't have time for such nonsense any more than I do, especially now that I'm single-handedly writing the next installment of our book.

How's that coming?

Beautifully, if I do say so myself. I'm having so much fun reading Weston's old letters.

Do I get to read them, too?

If you'll kindly deliver some potato soup to Seymour.

Olive, I'm sure they're feeding him at the hospital.

I know. But I want Seymour to know we're thinking about him. And I want him to read my notes for the new chapters.

I'll deliver it all tonight. I've rigged up a tray on a rope with pulleys.

You're brilliant, dear.

As brilliant as Weston Peece?

I'd have to think about that. Weston was a very clever fellow. What's this now? You're frowning.

I don't think I would've liked this Weston guy.

Of course you would have. Everyone loved Weston. You'll see what I mean when you read his letters.

Seymour,

Here's the next section.

Love,
Olive

43 Old Cemetery
Road

Weston and I
attended the same
one-room school-
house in Ghastly. We were
best friends, but that didn't stop us from
competing with each other for top academic honors.
Most years I won the writing and penmanship
awards. Weston took top honors in geography and
Latin.

W e always walked to school together, until
Weston got a horse when we were 17. Here's the
letter he wrote to tell me.

April 20, 1835

Dear Olive,

I guess you've seen my new horse. He's
plenty big enough for two people, so I'd be honored
if you'd let me pick you up and carry you to school.
I promise to ride carefully and deliver you safely—
mainly because I intend to defeat you in Friday's
spelling bee.

Yours truly,
Weston

I'm pleased to recall that *I* won the spelling bee. I won it by correctly spelling the word "ambition."

On the ride home from school that day, Weston asked what my ambition in life was.

"What's the one thing you want to do more than anything else on earth?" he asked.

After thinking for a minute about whether to take him into my confidence, I decided to trust Weston with my secret.

"I want to be an author," I said. "That is my great ambition in life."

As soon as the words left my lips, Weston jumped off the horse. He turned a cartwheel and said, "Olive, that's exactly what you should do— write books!"

I giggled, because I had occasional moments of shyness back then.

"I don't know if I will find success," I said, still sitting on the horse. "To be an author, you have to find someone willing to publish your books."

But Weston had enough confidence for both of us. "Publishers will battle for the privilege of printing your stories," he said, his arms raised dramatically. "Olive, you will be the most successful author in American history. And I will be your biggest fan."

Then he jumped back on the horse and we

rode the rest of the way home. We spent the after-noon reading together in front of my fireplace.

As Weston was leaving that day, I asked what *his* ambition in life was.

He smiled and narrowed his eyes. "Promise not to laugh?"

"I would never laugh at someone's ambition," I assured him.

"All right, then," he said. "I want to help people make friends through letters."

Such a lovely ambition for a lovely boy who was not only my best friend, but also, just a few years later, my mailman.

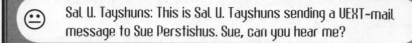

Sal U. Tayshuns: This is Sal U. Tayshuns sending a UEXT~mail message to Sue Perstishus. Sue, can you hear me?

Sue Perstishus: Yes, Mr. Tayshuns. And I should tell you that I have a customer here with me. His name is Mr. Grumply.

Sal U. Tayshuns: Our customers are always grumpy. But never mind that. The video component in my veil isn't working right. Is yours?

Sue Perstishus: Yes, sir. I can see you fine.

Sal U. Tayshuns: I don't care if you can see my behind. We have other business to discuss. Have you collected all the P.O. box keys in Ghastly?

Sue Perstishus: Yes. With the exception of one.

Sal U. Tayshuns: Care to tell me why?

Sue Perstishus: I'd rather not, sir. Not with Iggy here.

Sal U. Tayshuns: Ignore my icky hair. Now look, Sue, before we close the post office, you've gotta get keys from every customer who has a post office box in Ghastly. No exceptions.

Sue Perstishus: But there is an exception. It's a special case. I'd rather not discuss it.

Sal U. Tayshuns: Sue, may I remind you that a post office is federal property? If you don't tell me what this special case is, I'm going to send the FBI your way. They'll have you talking before I can say "parcel post."

Sue Perstishus [clears throat]: Okay, I'll tell you. There's a phantom living under the post office. He conducts his business from post office box 5.

Ignatius B. Grumply: A phantom? A real phantom?

Sue Perstishus: Yes, a real phantom.

Ignatius B. Grumply: Have you ever seen it?

Sue Perstishus: No. The phantom has never revealed his face to me. But sometimes I hear him crying. He cries the same sentence over and over in a sad voice: "I love Christine."

Sal U. Tayshuns: Well, I love crisp greens, too, Sue. But that's nothing to cry about. Fact is, I'm worried about you. I think the stress of transitioning to VEXT-mail is making you a little soft in the head. But don't worry. I've just decided something.

Sue Perstishus: What?

Sal U. Tayshuns: I'm going to come to Ghastly and help.

Sue Perstishus: Sir, I appreciate how understanding you are.

Sal U. Tayshuns: You can see my underwear? Sue, that's just plain inappropriate and you know it. But I'm going to ignore that remark because I have a hunch you're going through a rough patch and I want to help. What? Huh? I can't hear you. Oh, forget it. We'll talk when I get to Ghastly. Bye-bye, Sue.

Date: _February 7_

To: _Seymour Hope_
Room 5

Seymour,

R u awake? Whatcha doing?

I still have a fever and chills. And I miss my cell phone. 🙁

WY

Date: _February 7_

To: _Wynonna Fye_
Room 12

Dear Wy,

I miss my dog and cats. And I have the chills, too, but it might be from reading <u>The Phantom of the Opera.</u> It's really good! Here's the story so far.

A creepy phantom lives under the Paris Opera House. He's really mad because the new manager of the opera is trying to take away his private box seat. The phantom sends the manager an angry letter with these words: "I want to keep box seat 5, and I want the lovely Christine to be the star of the opera. If you ignore my demands, something terrible will happen!"

Rats. Dr. Dedyet just came in and said I have to turn off my reading light at midnight. That's only ten minutes away. Oh well, I'll read more tomorrow and keep you posted on the story.

Goodnight, Wy.

    —Seymour

P.S. One week down, three weeks to go before you get your phone back. Hang in there, pal!

IGNATIUS B. GRUMPLY

A WRITER IN RESIDENCE

43 OLD CEMETERY ROAD   2ND FLOOR   GHASTLY, ILLINOIS

February 7

Sue Perstishus
Postmaster, Ghastly Post Office
2 Dead Letter Drive
Ghastly, Illinois

Dear Sue,

If I could figure out how to use the cell phone that
M. Balm lent me, I would call you. But given the
fact that it's almost midnight, perhaps it's best
that I write you a letter instead to express my
concerns about what you said yesterday.

For the past six weeks, I too have had a funny
feeling about post office box 5. The letters we've
received bearing that address have been strange,
baffling, and even threatening. The most recent
note threatened to steal a letter at midnight.

For the life of me, I couldn't figure out what that
meant. But when I heard you tell Sal U. Tayshuns
about a phantom, a *real* phantom, who conducts
his business from

Oh, Iggy. Phor pity's sake, are you still phixated on . . . Well, phiddlesticks. I can't seem to phind the letter that comes aphter "e."

Good heavens, it's happened! He's stolen a letter—phrom the alphabet!

Don't be phoolish. How could someone lipht a letter phrom the alphabet?

I don't know, but he did, just as he warned he would. And look at the time: It's exactly midnight. Olive, our phan is a phantom!

I don't believe it. Phantoms are phound only in phiction.

Then how do you explain those phan letters and now this philched letter?

I'd say it's the work oph a phake, a phraud, or a phlim-phlam man. Oh, phooey! Let's just phorget about this phor now. I'm sure by morning everything will be phine.

➤THE GHASTLY TIMES◄

Sunday, Phebruary 8
Cliph Hanger, Editor

"We're Living in Ghastly Times"

$1.50
Morning Edition

Phorgive Our Phonts

A strange virus has inphected our computer system. We pheel phairly certain we'll have the problem phixed soon. So don't phret. We think it's just a phluke.

Phantom Phlu Update

Seymour Hope and Wynonna "Wy" Phye can read scary books, pass silly notes and stay up till midnight.

But the two young patients diagnosed with phantom phlu can't leave their hospital beds until their phevers break.

"Both patients are pheeling much better," said Dr. Izzy Dedyet. "But just to be saphe, I plan to keep them quarantined until they have been phree oph phevers phor 24 hours. I don't want anyone else to catch this pherocious phlu."

In the meantime Hope and Phye are keeping themselves entertained with interesting reading material. "They've been reading the daily newspaper, *The Phantom oph the Opera* and even some oph Olive C. Spence's old letters," said Dedyet. "The kids say they love reading about Olive's old phriend Weston Peece."

**Hope enjoys special deliveries
in the hospital.**

Dr. Dedyet added that he did not object to the delivery system Ignatius B. Grumply has rigged up outside his son's hospital window. "It's a nice distraction phor both Seymour and Wynonna, who I'm pleased to say is also recovering nicely phrom her cell phone phetish," said Dedyet.

Phoggy Phuture phor *43 Old Cemetery Road*

Phor months now the creators oph *43 Old Cemetery Road* have delivered new chapters oph their bestselling ghost story to subscribers by U.S. mail. But what will become oph *43 Old Cemetery Road* when the Ghastly Post Ophice closes phorever on Phebruary 28?

"I haven't the phoggiest notion," said Ignatius B. Grumply.

Asked iph he and his coauthor, Olive C. Spence, had considered the option oph using VEXT-mail, Grumply grunted. "Olive doesn't believe in modern technology, and I can't even turn on a simple cell phone. It's so phrustrating!"

Equally phrustrating, says Grumply, is the phact that the chapters in progress are possibly their best yet. "Olive has been digging out her old letters phrom Weston Peece, her liphelong phriend," said Grumply. "His letters demonstrate the power

(Continued on page 2, column 1)

PHUTURE *(Continued phrom page 1, column 2)*

Grumply phinds diphiculties phar phrom phunny.

oph the written word and the magic oph phriendships phormed through old-phashioned letters. But without the post ophice, how can we possibly share this phine story with our phans? Iph this weren't so bitterly ironic, it might be phunny."

Don't Phorget!

Beginning March 1, mail service will be replaced by VEXT~mail.

Sal U. Tayshuns Here to Phind Out a Phew Phacts

U.S. Postmaster General Sal U. Tayshuns arrived in Ghastly yesterday to oversee the transition phrom regular mail to VEXT-mail.

"I realize this might seem like a phrightening change phor many people, especially older pholks who aren't comphortable with new-phangled technology," said Tayshuns. "That's why I'm here to phacilitate the transition."

Oph special concern to Tayshuns is phiguring out whether Ghastly Postmaster Sue Perstishus is competent to serve as the nation's phirst VEXTmaster. "I have a phew concerns on that phront," conphessed Tayshuns.

His other phocus is the one remaining resident of Ghastly who thus phar has rephused to surrender the key to his post ophice box, number 5.

"I'm sure he's a phine phellow," said Tayshuns. "I'm conphident we can resolve this in a phriendly way, phace to phace."

Sue Perstishus isn't so sure. "Phrankly, I'm not certain the phantom has a phace," she said. "Iph he does, I've never seen it."

Wait. *The phantom?*

"That's right," said Perstishus phirmly.

"I've kept the secret long enough. There's a phantom haunting the Ghastly Post Ophice. Every night he cries, 'I love Christine.'"

"Now do you see why I'm concerned about Sue?" said Tayshuns, looking phrazzled. "Next thing she's going to say is that she believes in ghosts!"

Tayshuns is staying at the Ghastly Inn while in town.

Sal U. Tayshuns phinds phault with Perstishus.

Sal U. Tayshuns
U.S. Postmaster General
VEXT-mail address: Salutayshuns@vextmail.123µøÇ¥Å

The Ghastly Inn, Room 5
99 Cophin Avenue
Ghastly, Illinois

Phebruary 9

Ms. Sue Perstishus
Postmaster, Ghastly Post Ophice
2 Dead Letter Drive
Ghastly, Illinois

Dear Sue,

I'm sorry it's come to this, but I'm going to have to let you go. It's obvious this new VEXT-mail technology is too much phor you. And it's my responsibility to relieve you oph your duties here in Ghastly bephore your brain becomes, well, let's just say *phried*.

That's the bad news. The good news is, I'm not going to phire you. I'm going to transpher you to a relaxing little post at the Grand Canyon called

Phantom Ranch. How's that phor a coincidence? And here's the best part. Do you know how mail is delivered to Phantom Ranch? By mules trained on a pharm in Phlorida! Doesn't that sound like phun? I think the phresh air will suit you just phine. And don't worry. I will phill in as our nation's phirst VEXTmaster until I can phind someone else.

So, Sue, iph you would just sign the enclosed transpher phorm, we'll have you delivering mail by mule phaster than you can say "phirst class."

Sincerely yours,

Sal U. Tayshuns

Sal U. Tayshuns

P.S. Don't know what's gotten into the spellcheck phunction on my laptop. No wonder the printed word is doomed. It's too phinicky.

UNITED STATES POSTAL SERVICE
TRANSPHER PHORM

Name: __Sue Perstishus__

Home post ophice: __Ghastly, Illinois__

Transpher post ophice: __Phantom Ranch, Arizona__

Date oph transpher: __March 1__

Reasons phor transpher: __Stress, incompetence,__
__and delusions oph a phantom residing under__
__Ghastly Post Ophice__

Transpherring Ophicial: __Sal V. Tayphuns__

Transpherred Employee: _____

Sign phirmly
here,
Sue

Waiver oph Responsibility
Please note that all job transphers are contingent on the
continuation oph regular mail delivery.
In the event that new technology
or devices, whether existing now or in the phuture,
eliminate the need phor mail delivery services,
this job shall likewise be eliminated.
We apologize phor any inconvenience
this might cause
you, your phriends,
or your
phamily.

Sue Perstishus

Postmaster, Ghastly Post Ophice

2 Dead Letter Drive   Ghastly, Illinois

Phebruary 10

Sal U. Tayshuns
c/o The Ghastly Inn
99 Cophin Avenue
Ghastly, Illinois

Dear Mr. Tayshuns,

Phonts and phunctions may be phinicky, but the written
word is the phoundation oph democracy and phreedom.
Anyway, that's my belieph.

As phor my transpher, no thank you. I have no desire
to deliver mail by mules raised on a Phlorida pharm.
But I would like you to know that I am dephinitely *not*
delusional. There is a phantom living under the Ghastly
Post Ophice. Iph you don't believe me, you can contact
him yourselph by letter. That's the phantom's prepherred
phorm oph communication.

Yours phorever committed to the written word,

Sue Perstishus

Sue Perstishus

Sal U. Tayshuns
U.S. Postmaster General

VEXT-mail address: Salutayshuns@vextmail.123µøÇ¥Å

PHINAL AND OPHICIAL NOTICE   **DO NOT IGNORE!**

Phebruary 11

Occupant
P.O. Box 5
Ghastly, Illinois

Dear Occupant:

Perhaps you are unaware oph the phact that beginning on March 1, you will not be able to receive mail in your post ophice box.

You will, however, be able to communicate phaster and more ephiciently with VEXT-mail, which, as a special phavor to you, I am making available phor PHREE phor the phirst year.

So please take a phew minutes to come in and exchange your P.O. box key phor a VEXT-mail veil. I have every conphidence that you will enjoy this phancy new phorm oph communication.

Sincerely,

Sal U. Tayshuns

Sal U. Tayshuns

P.S. I apologize phor my spelling errors. Phor the liphe oph me I can't phigure out how to get the spellcheck phunction to work on my laptop here at The Ghastly Inn. Must be some sort oph phleeting malphunction.

P.O. BOX 5
GHASTLY, ILLINOIS

GHASTLY
AM
PHEB 12
·IL·

MR. SAL U. TAYSHUNS
C/O THE GHASTLY INN
99 COPHIN AVENUE
GHASTLY, ILLINOIS

P.O. BOX 5
GHASTLY, ILLINOIS

PHEBRUARY 12

MR. TAYSHUNS:

I REPHUSE TO SURRENDER MY KEY TO
P.O. BOX 5. AND I STRONGLY SUGGEST
YOU ABANDON YOUR MISSION.

YOURS TRULY,

THE PHAN

P.S. <u>OPH COURSE</u> SUE PERSTISHUS
BELIEVES IN GHOSTS. EVERYONE IN
GHASTLY DOES, YOU PHOOL!

Sal U. Tayshuns
U.S. Postmaster General

UEXT-mail address: Salutayshuns@uextmail.123µøÇ¥Å

Phebruary 13

Occupant
P.O. Box 5
Ghastly, Illinois

Dear Occupant:

Did you repher to me as a phool? Phine. No more mister nice guy.

Tomorrow I will hold a press conpherence to announce my revised plans phor the Ghastly Post Ophice.

Phrom,

Sal U. Tayshuns

Sal U. Tayshuns

PRESS RELEASE

Phor Immediate Release
Phebruary 14

POST OPHICE TO BE DEMOLISHED
ON MARCH PHIRST

(GHASTLY, ILLINOIS) In the interest oph public saphety, the Ghastly Post Ophice will be demolished on March 1 and replaced with a mobile VEXT-mail center.

"Old buildings are as useless as old-phashioned letters," said U.S. Postmaster General Sal U. Tayshuns. "It only makes sense that we demolish the Ghastly Post Ophice as a way to symbolize the end oph an old, outdated phorm oph communication."

A mobile VEXT-mail center will open in Ghastly on March 1, just minutes aphter the demolition oph the Ghastly Post Ophice. "The VEXT-mail center will be inphlatable," said Tayshuns. "I can assemble it myselph in phiphteen minutes phlat."

Ghastly will be the phirst U.S. city to replace regular mail with VEXT-mail. Tayshuns is in Ghastly overseeing the transition. "Everyone here thinks it'll be phun and phantastic," said Tayshuns. "Well, almost everyone."

PRESS RELEASE

FOR IMMEDIATE RELEASE
FEBRUARY 15

<u>PHANTOM TO STRIKE ONE LAST TIME</u>

IN THE INTEREST OF CLARITY, I AM RETURN-
ING THE LETTER "F" TO ITS RIGHTFUL PLACE
IN THE ALPHABET.

BUT BE WARNED: I WILL STRIKE ONE LAST
TIME, AND I WILL WIN.

YOURS TRULY,

THE PHANTOM

IGNATIUS B. GRUMPLY

A WRITER IN RESIDENCE

43 OLD CEMETERY ROAD　　　　**2ND FLOOR**　　　　**GHASTLY, ILLINOIS**

February 16

The Phantom
P.O. Box 5
Ghastly, Illinois

Dear Sir,

I am writing with great haste. Olive doesn't believe
you exist. But I do. Who are you and what do you
want?

With grave sincerity,

Ignatius B. Grumply

Ignatius B. Grumply

P.S. Thanks for returning the letter "f." It's always
been my favorite.

P.O. BOX 5
GHASTLY, ILLINOIS

FEBRUARY 17

IGNATIUS B. GRUMPLY
43 OLD CEMETERY ROAD
GHASTLY, ILLINOIS

DEAR IGNATIUS,

WHO I AM IS NO CONCERN OF YOURS. BUT
WHAT I WANT IS SIMPLE: I WANT TO SEE
OLIVE BEFORE THE POST OFFICE IS
DESTROYED.

BRING HER TO ME ON THE LAST DAY OF
FEBRUARY AT ONE MINUTE BEFORE MID-
NIGHT. I'LL BE WAITING AT P.O. BOX 5.

YOURS TRULY,

THE PHANTOM

O.C.S.

Ghost Writer in Residence
43 Old Cemetery Road, The Cupola
Ghastly, Illinois

February 20

Seymour Hope
Greater Ghastly Memorial Hospital
4 Morgue Way
Ghastly, Illinois

Dear Seymour,

I don't know where Iggy is. Your father has not
been himself lately. I blame that silly telephone
he's been carrying in his pocket for weeks. It's made
him terribly distracted.

Well, I suppose I shall just have to deliver your
lunch tray myself. Enjoy the soup, darling. I'll also
include some reading material. I had hoped to cre-
ate three new chapters of our book from Weston's
old letters. But now that I've come to his final correspondence, I don't think that's possible. The ending is too depressing.

You'll see what I mean when you read it.

Love,

Olive

43 Old Cemetery Road

While I pursued my ambition of becoming a published author, Weston became Ghastly's first postmaster and mail carrier.

He sorted letters in the morning and delivered them in the afternoon from his horse-drawn carriage. We spent most evenings together, reading in front of the fire. But even so, we still wrote letters to each other, just as we'd done as children.

October 24, 1901

Dear Olive,

Thank you for leaving the apple cake and milk for me in your mailbox. That is not the intended purpose of a mailbox, but I was certainly hungry by the time I got to Old Cemetery Road. And who else would be thoughtful enough to leave me an afternoon snack? Only you, Olive.

I hope to repay your kindness the day I deliver an acceptance letter to you from a New York publisher. You're the most talented writer in the whole world, so please don't be discouraged that no publisher has accepted your stories yet. Someone will. And I am so pleased that I'll be the person who gets to deliver the good news to you.

Until then, I remain

Yours truly,

Weston

But as everyone knows, I never published a book during my lifetime. My manuscripts were rejected by every publisher in New York City.

Was I disappointed? Yes. Heartbroken? Indeed. Did I die a failure? I'm afraid so. But at least I had Weston's letters to keep my spirits up.

I was on my deathbed when I received this one.

May 4, 1911

Dear Olive,

I'm sorry I've been so slow on my route this week. I'm afraid I'm not feeling very good. One minute I'm quite warm. The next minute I'm chilled. Must be this foul weather.

I know neither one of us is getting younger, Olive. And I'm sorry that every year I get a little slower in delivering your mail.

Everyone says I should retire, but they don't know what keeps me going: the thought that one day I will have the honor of delivering an acceptance letter to you. Won't we have a fine party then?

Yours truly,
Weston

I died the very next day. After years of waiting, I never received an acceptance letter for my work.

IGNATIUS B. GRUMPLY

A WRITER IN RESIDENCE

43 OLD CEMETERY ROAD   2ND FLOOR   GHASTLY, ILLINOIS

February 21

Olive C. Spence
The Cupola
43 Old Cemetery Road
Ghastly, Illinois

Dear Olive,

I have so much to tell you, I don't know where to
begin. With the good news of Seymour's improved
health? The bad news of the scheduled demolition
of the post office? Or the unbelievable news that a
phantom—yes, a phantom!—lives in Ghastly and
occupies P.O. box 5? I know you'll find this hard to
believe, but I've been in contact with the phantom
of the post office. At first I didn't think it could be
true, but I've been camped outside the post office
the past two nights listening to him cry and

Blah blah blah.

Olive! I wish you wouldn't startle me like that.

And I wish you wouldn't be so dramatic.

What do you mean?

Oh, it's not your fault. I'm afraid I lived my whole life under the spell of the post office.

What on earth are you saying?

Iggy, listen to me. There is nothing beautiful or magical about old-fashioned letters. I've been dead wrong to romanticize the cruel practice of letter writing.

How can you possibly say that?

Because I've had a change of heart, that's how! In rereading those old letters from Weston I've realized what terrible pain the post office caused me during my lifetime. To think of all those years I spent waiting for an acceptance letter from a publishing company, telling me that my stories were worthy of publication. Can you imagine the utter heartache of never receiving the *one* letter you really wanted?

But Olive, as a ghost you've become a world-famous author.

Too little, too late. I'm done with letters—forever. And I will dance on the grave of the Ghastly Post Office.

3

You can't mean that you support the demolition of the post office.

Oh, can't I? Step aside while I write my last letter.

➤THE GHASTLY TIMES➤

Sunday, February 22
Cliff Hanger, Editor

"We're Living in Ghastly Times"

$1.50
Morning Edition

"Let's Have a Wrecking Ball," says Olive C. Spence
Ghastly's ghost proposes party
to "celebrate" post office demolition

**A wrecking ball stands on the site of
Saturday night's Wrecking Ball.**

Who would've thought it?

Olive C. Spence, Ghastly's beloved
ghost and bestselling author, has thrown her
full support behind the demolition of the
Ghastly Post Office.

In a letter to this newspaper (see side
story), Spence explains her reasons for pro-
posing a Wrecking Ball to celebrate the
death of the old-fashioned letter.

Reaction to the news has been strong.

"You could've knocked me over with a
feather when I heard Miss Spence was finished with writing letters," said M. Balm.
"She's made a fine art of letter writing."

Sue Perstishus described the news as
disappointing. Even Spence's coauthor,
Ignatius B. Grumply, seemed shaken by
Spence's dramatic U-turn.

"Olive claims to have fallen under the
spell of the post office," Grumply said. "I
don't know what she means by that. And I
don't know how we can continue our book

(Continued on page 2, column 1)

The Last Letter of Olive C. Spence

Dear friends,

Think of all the bad news that
arrives by letter. Then think of all
the good news that never arrives.
Then consider all the junk mail.
It's high time we do away with
the savage practice of writing letters!

To this end, I offer my full
support of the closing of the Ghastly
Post Office. And I propose a grand
party to celebrate the end of this
grim chapter of human existence.

As the wrecking ball prepares
to demolish the post office, let's have
a Wrecking Ball. Please dress in
your finest evening clothes and meet
outside the main entrance of the
Ghastly Post Office on Saturday
night, February 28. We will say
good-bye and good riddance to the
written word.

Yours as I sign my very last letter,

Olive Christine Spence

P.S. A sincere thank-you to Sue
Perstishus for her decades of supe-
rior postal service. My decision is no
reflection on you, Sue, or your postal
predecessors.

BALL *(Continued from page 1, column 1)*
given the fact that it's composed mainly of letters and delivered to readers by the U.S. Postal Service. I'm not even sure how Olive and I will continue to communicate."

By contrast, U.S. Postmaster General Sal U. Tayshuns says Spence is dead right. "Thank goodness someone in this town understands what I'm trying to do," Tayshuns stated. "I'm eager to meet Miss Spence at the Wrecking Ball. She sounds like my kind of twenty-first-century gal!"

When told by Sue Perstishus that Olive C. Spence is the ghost of a woman who died in 1911, Tayshuns shook his head sadly. "Poor old Sue," he said. "Her nougat's a little gooey, if you know what I mean."

The Wrecking Ball will be held outside the main entrance to the post office. Everyone in Ghastly is invited.

Patients Improving with Time, Tales

Hope and Fye continue to improve under doctor's care.

Much better but not well enough to be released.

That's how Dr. Izzy Dedyet described Seymour Hope and Wynonna "Wy" Fye, the two young patients hospitalized with phantom flu at Greater Ghastly Memorial Hospital.

"Their conditions have stabilized," said Dr. Dedyet. "But their temperatures are still both a bit high."

Until their temperatures return to normal, Dr. Dedyet said Hope and Fye are enjoying *The Phantom of the Opera*. "It's a real thriller," said Dedyet, who gets a daily plot summary from his patients. "We all loved when the phantom appeared at the masquerade party. Now we're at the part where the phantom has kidnapped his love, Christine. Wy says it's getting creepier with every page."

Date: <u>February 22</u>

To: <u>Wynonna Fye</u>
    <u>Room 12</u>

Dear Wy,

Did you get today's newspaper with your breakfast tray? It's so weird. Olive told me when you're tired of writing letters, you're tired of life. If she's giving up on writing letters, I won't be able to talk to her anymore. This is terrible. ☹

The only thing cheering me up is the picture of you in the newspaper. You're really cute.

Sincerely,

　　　—Seymour

Date: February 22

To: Seymour Hope
Room 5

Seymour,

Forget cute. This is serious stuff! Think about it:

The Phantom of the Opera	The Phantom of the Post Office
Haunts the Paris Opera House	Haunts the Ghastly Post Office
Conducts business from box seat #5	Conducts business from post office box 5
Is in love with the singer Christine	Is in love with the writer Olive <u>Christine</u> Spence
<u>Kidnapped</u> Christine	?!?!

Don't you get it, Seymour? The phantom of the post office plans to kidnap Olive Christine Spence!

If I had my cell phone, I could call my uncle and tell him everything. But I don't, so there's only one thing left for us to do: We <u>have</u> to go to the Wrecking Ball. We have to save Olive from the phantom of the post office!

The only question is HOW. Any ideas?

WY

Date: <u>February 22</u>

To: <u>Wynonna Fye</u>
<u>Room 12</u>

Dear Wy,

Yes! I know exactly how we can save Olive. Meet me
in my room at 11:30 on Saturday night. Just don't
let Dr. Dedyet see you. He might not approve of my
escape plan.

—Seymour

P.S. You're not only cute—you're also the smartest person in this hospital. I'm excited we're finally going to
meet face to face.

Sue Perstishus

Postmaster, Ghastly Post Office
2 Dead Letter Drive   Ghastly, Illinois

February 22

Mr. Sal U. Tayshuns
c/o The Ghastly Inn
99 Coffin Avenue
Ghastly, Illinois

Dear Mr. Tayshuns,

I read what you said about me in the newspaper. Believe it or not, I don't mind if you think I'm nutty. Why? Because I know for a *fact* that a phantom is living under the Ghastly Post Office. And I worry about what he will do when you demolish his home.

As for VEXT-mail, I now feel at liberty to tell you exactly what I think of it. It's a ridiculous technology that will *never* be accepted by the people of Ghastly. I'm just warning you.

Also, please know that I plan to serve as postmaster of Ghastly until March 1. Wrecking ball or no wrecking ball, I will be at my post defending the written word until the bitter end.

Sincerely dedicated,

Sue Perstishus

Sue Perstishus

Sal U. Tayshuns
U.S. Postmaster General

VEXT-mail address: Salutayshuns@vextmail.123µøÇ¥Å

February 23

Sue Perstishus
Postmaster, Ghastly Post Office
2 Dead Letter Drive
Ghastly, Illinois

Dear Sue,

See? This is what I'm talking about. Here you have a perfect opportunity to use VEXT-mail to contact me. But what do you do? Write a blasted letter.

Well, Sue, have it your way for a few more days. On March 1, there will *be* no more letters in this town. There will be only VEXT-mail.

Speaking of warnings: I think I should warn *you* that the wrecking ball crew is scheduled to destroy the post office at one minute after midnight on March 1. If you are inside the post office at 12:01 A.M., you will be as dead as the written word.

Sincerely,

Sal U. Tayshuns

Sal U. Tayshuns

P.S. I wish you'd told me about Olive C. Spence. I want to give that gal a free VEXT-mail veil. Maybe I can even talk her into being Ghastly's first VEXTmaster. Do you know her address?

February 24

Mr. Sal U. Tayshuns
c/o The Ghastly Inn
99 Coffin Avenue
Ghastly, Illinois

Dear Mr. Tayshuns,

Olive's address is 43 Old Cemetery Road. I dare you to contact her.

Sincerely,

Sue Perstishus

Sue Perstishus

Sal U. Tayshuns
U.S. Postmaster General
VEXT-mail address: Salutayshuns@vextmail.123µøÇ¥Å

February 25

Olive C. Spence
43 Old Cemetery Road
Ghastly, Illinois

Dear Miss Spence,

Just a friendly note from one technology lover to another
to let you know that I'm looking forward to meeting you
at the Wrecking Ball on Saturday night. What a great
idea to celebrate the demolition of the post office and the
death of the letter! I only wish I'd thought of it. Ha ha!

Anyhoo, in recognition of your fine work in promoting
VEXT-mail, I'd like to offer you a free VEXT-mail veil and
a coupon for six months of free VEXTing. Please redeem
your coupon at the Wrecking Ball. I'll see you there!

Sincerely,

Sal U. Tayshuns

Sal U. Tayshuns

February 26

Ignatius B. Grumply
43 Old Cemetery Road
Ghastly, Illinois

Dear Mr. Grumply,

Never in all my born days did I think I'd see the death of good old-fashioned letters. And to think Olive C. Spence is supporting this! I started to write her a letter asking why but realized I'd never hear back from her.

And poor Sue Perstishus. This whole VEXT-mail thing has clearly thrown her for a loop. Sue's always been the nervous type, but now all this talk of a *phantom?* It must be giving her a nervous breakdown.

Well, I don't know about you, but I refuse to attend the Wrecking Ball. I plan to spend Saturday night at home, reading some of my favorite old letters. I'm just glad Wy and Seymour are safe in the hospital and not forced to witness this sad turn of events.

The only good thing that's happened this month is that Dr. Dedyet tells me my niece has almost completely kicked her cell phone habit. If Wy can make it to March 1, she'll have gone a full month without using her phone. I only wish she could have made a friend or two while she was in town. Maybe next time.

Speaking of Wy, I'll need to get her phone back from you so that I can return it to her before she leaves town on March 1. Please feel free to use it until then to keep in touch with Seymour.

I wish I could think of something more interesting to write given the fact that this is likely the last letter I'll ever mail. But perhaps it's best to sign off with just a simple description of how I'm feeling.

Sincerely sad,

M. Balm

IGNATIUS B. GRUMPLY

A WRITER IN RESIDENCE

43 OLD CEMETERY ROAD   2ND FLOOR   GHASTLY, ILLINOIS

February 27

M. Balm
Ghastly Public Library
12 Scary Street
Ghastly, Illinois

Dear Mr. Balm,

You are a man of great integrity and I respect
your decision *not* to attend the Wrecking Ball.
The matter is a bit more complicated for me.

The fact is, there *is* a phantom of the post office.
And Olive is playing right into his hands. He
wants to meet her inside the post office tomorrow night at one minute before midnight. I don't
know if Olive realizes the danger she's in, or if
she saw the letter we received in today's mail.
(See enclosed.)

I keep thinking there must be some connection
between these sinister letters and the demise
of the post office, but I can't figure it out. In
any case, this is indeed a sad day for Ghastly.

Like you, I'm grateful that your niece and my son are safely in the hospital and out of harm's way. Now if I can just think of a way to keep Olive safe.

Sincerely terrified, confused, and maybe a tiny bit fluish,

I Gnatius B. Grumply

Ignatius B. Grumply

P.S. I will be happy to return your niece's phone on March 1. I'm embarrassed to admit I still haven't figured out how to use it. But I shall continue to carry it with me, just in case.

P.O. BOX 5
GHASTLY, ILLINOIS

FEBRUARY 26

DEAR OLIVE AND IGNATIUS,

SEE YOU SATURDAY NIGHT.

YOURS TRULY,

A FAN

Greater Ghastly Memorial Hospital

4 Morgue Way
Ghastly, Illinois

Date: February 28

To: Seymour Hope
Room 5

Dear Seymour,

Are you almost ready? I am. But I'm worried about one thing: If we're still contagious, do you think we should really leave the hospital?

WY

Date: February 28

To: Wynonna Fye
      Room 12

Dear Wy,

Don't worry. I have surgical masks for us and blankets, too, in case we get chilled.

I also have a theory about who the phantom of the post office is. I'll tell you when we meet face to face—or mask to mask.

—Seymour

February 28

Olive C. Spence
The Cupola
43 Old Cemetery Road
Ghastly, Illinois

Dear Olive,

It's 11:45 P.M. The house is as quiet as a tomb.
I'm not sure if you're here or not. If you are, please
listen to me.

I *don't* want you to go to the post office tonight.
You're in real danger, Olive. There's a phantom
waiting for you.

Did I just hear you chuckle—or was that the wind?
I feel a bit dizzy. Maybe a little warm, too. The
truth is, I'm sick with worry. Are you still here,
Olive? Are you reading over my shoulder as you
usually do? To think how I used to complain about
the way you interrupted my letters. Now I would
kick up my heels with joy if you would add so much
as one word to this letter.

But you've given up on letters, haven't you? That means you've given up on life. And on the afterlife. And on me and Seymour. Oh, Olive. Are you even still here?

Wait! I just heard the front door slam. You've left, haven't you? Are you going to the post office? You must be! I'm right behind you!

Yours to the rescue,

IGnatius

Sal U. Tayshuns: This is Sal U. Tayshuns, welcoming everyone to the Wrecking Ball. It's not often I get a chance to wear a tuxedo. I clean up pretty well, don't I, folks?

[Sound of applause from crowd]

Sal U. Tayshuns: Well, fancy clothes aside, it's an honor to gather together outside the post office and celebrate the end of old-fashioned letters and the beginning of this exciting new chapter in communications. I know you're all wondering how UEXT-mail works, so watch closely. See how I have my UEXT-mail veil pulled snugly over my head? If I want to make a call, all I have to do is click this button here. See? Hello, Sue? Can you hear me?

Sue Perstishus: Yes, sir. I can hear you. I can see you, too.

Sal U. Tayshuns: Perfect! Can you believe this, folks? Sue's inside the post office and we're outside. But I can see and talk to her with my UEXT-mail veil. Isn't this terrific?

[Sound of applause from crowd]

Sue Perstishus: Well, I think it's the end of civilization.

Sal U. Tayshuns: I don't think it's a silly nation, Sue. I think this is a flat-out fantabulous nation. And I'm proud to call myself an American when I see the kind of technological advances we make every day in this great country.

Sue Perstishus: You misunderstood me, sir. But I don't care. All of Ghastly will soon learn how worthless and unreliable these veils are.

Sal U. Tayshuns: A stale cigar? There you go again, Sue, talking nonsense.

Sue, I'm worried about you in there.

Sal U. Tayshuns: Who's that? Who's joined this conversation?

Sue Perstishus: Miss Spence, is that really you?

Yes, And I fully support the demolition of the post office. But I don't want you to get hurt in the process, dear. Do you realize there's a dangerous wrecking ball right outside your door?

Sue Perstishus: I do. But I will not leave my post until my term as postmaster expires at midnight.

But that's only two minutes away. You could be killed.

Sal U. Tayshuns. Is this really Olive C. Spence? If so, I have a VEXT-mail veil for you.

You really are a ninny, aren't you, Mr. Sal U. Tayshuns? I don't need a veil to communicate.

Sal U. Tayshuns: Oh, now I see you. What interesting opera glasses you have. They appear to float. And are you wearing an invisibility cloak?

Sue Perstishus: She's a ghost, sir. She doesn't need a cloak to be invisible. Miss Spence, I appreciate your concern for my safety. I promise I will leave the post office at twelve o'clock on the dot.

That's cutting it awfully close. I'm coming in to get you.

[Ignatius B. Grumply arrives, breathless]

Ignatius B. Grumply: Olive, don't go inside! It's too dangerous.

Don't worry about me, Iggy. I can't be hurt by a wrecking ball. I'm already dead, remember?

Ignatius B. Grumply: It's not the wrecking ball I'm worried about. It's the—

No time to chat, Iggy. Sue's in danger. I have to get her out before the wrecking ball takes aim at the post office. I'll be back in a flash.

[Olive C. Spence goes inside post office]

🙂 Ignatius B. Grumply: If you're going in, I'm going in, too.

[Ignatius B. Grumply goes inside post office]

😐 Sal U. Tayshuns: Sue, are you still there?

😊 Sue Perstishus: I am, sir. And now Miss Spence and Mr. Grumply have joined me.

😐 Sal U. Tayshuns: Turn your veil around, Sue. Ah, now I can see you all.

[Post office box 5 creaks open; a masked creature emerges with a letter]

🙂 Sal U. Tayshuns: Who's that?

Yes, who is that?

ME.

Who are you? And why are you wearing that silly mask?

BECAUSE I DON'T WANT TO SHOW MY FACE.

☹️ Ignatius B. Grumply: Olive, be very careful. It's the phantom of the post office.

Sal U. Tayshuns: Did someone say *phantom*? I see those strange floating opera glasses. And now I see an odd figure with a mask over his face.

Sue Perstishus: He's here at last. The phantom from P.O. box 5!

The person who sent those fan letters? I'd like to know who you are. Identify yourself at once!

I'M TOO ASHAMED TO TELL YOU WHO I AM.

[Seymour Hope and Wy Fye enter wrapped in blankets and wearing surgical masks]

Seymour Hope: We know!

Wy Fye: Yeah, Seymour figured it out.

Seymour Hope: We both figured it out.

Sal U. Tayshuns: Now I see the floating glasses, one large masked creature, and two smaller creatures with mysterious cloaks and masks.

Seymour Hope: Remove your mask, Mr. Peece!

IF YOU INSIST.

[The phantom removes his mask]

Weston? Weston Peece? Is that you? Where have you been all these years?

HIDING IN THE BASEMENT OF THE POST OFFICE.

Why?

BECAUSE I LET YOU DOWN.

What on earth are you talking about?

I FAILED TO DELIVER A LETTER TO YOU THAT MIGHT'VE SAVED YOUR LIFE.

[The phantom hands Olive a letter; Olive opens it]

What's this? An acceptance letter—for me? From a publishing company in France? Weston, this letter is postmarked 1911.

IT ARRIVED THE DAY YOU DIED, BUT I DIDN'T DELIVER IT TO YOU IN TIME. IF ONLY I HAD GOTTEN THE LETTER TO YOU SOONER, OLIVE, IT MIGHT'VE SAVED YOUR

LIFE. BUT I WAS MOVING SO
SLOWLY THAT DAY. I DIDN'T FEEL
LIKE MYSELF. I DON'T KNOW WHY.

Wy Fye: I know why, Mr. Peece. You had the flu.

THE FLU?

Seymour Hope: I bet you called it influenza back in your day.
But from the symptoms you describe, you probably had
the flu.

Wy Fye: So it's not your fault you couldn't deliver the letter.
You were sick.

AND TO THINK ALL THESE YEARS
I THOUGHT I DIED FROM THE
GUILT OF NOT DELIVERING THAT
ACCEPTANCE LETTER BEFORE
OLIVE'S DEATH.

Oh, Weston. You were always such a
sensitive soul.

Ignatius B. Grumply: Do you two need some private time?

Yes, but first things first. Mr. Sal U.
Tayshuns, are you still there?

Sal U. Tayshuns: Wha wha wha . . . Now I . . . I . . . I feel a bit faint and somewhat befuddled.

Then listen closely. This post office is not closing tonight, tomorrow, or ever. Do you understand me? This post office will remain open forevermore.

Sal U. Tayshuns: I . . . uh . . . wha wha wha . . . [CLONK]

[Sal U. Tayshuns faints]

Seymour Hope: Mr. Peece, maybe you couldn't deliver Olive's acceptance letter, but you saved the post office.

WITH YOUR HELP, SEYMOUR.

Ignatius B. Grumply: I think we have three new chapters for our book, if Mr. Peece will allow us to tell his story.

IT WOULD BE MY GREAT HONOR. AND PLEASE, CALL ME WESTON.

Oh, Weston, you dear, sweet man. Uh-oh. What was that sound?

Seymour Hope: The wrecking ball. Oh my gosh, it just bashed in the front door! We're trapped! We're all going to die!

Ignatius B. Grumply: Don't worry. We can call for help. I have a cell phone. Let me just figure out how to turn the stupid thing on. Hold on. Give me a minute.

Wy Fye: Is that my phone?

Seymour Hope: Wy, wait! You can't use it. You have just one minute to go to win your bet with your uncle.

Wy Fye: I don't care. Give me that thing!

➤THE GHASTLY TIMES➤

Sunday, March 1
Cliff Hanger, Editor

"We're Living in Ghastly Times"

$1.50
Afternoon Edition

OMG!
Wy's Text Message Saves the Day *and* the Post Office

A timely text message allows narrow escape at Wrecking Ball.

She claims she couldn't have done it without her cell phone—or her uncle.

But the fact is it was Wynonna "Wy" Fye's quick thinking combined with her just-in-time text message that saved several people, including Miss Fye herself, from almost certain death at the Ghastly Post Office shortly after midnight.

"I knew I had to get someone to call off the wrecking ball," said Fye. "Otherwise, we all would've been buried alive."

M. Balm, chief librarian at the Ghastly Public Library, was on the receiving end of the text message. "As soon as I read it, I called the police," said Balm. "And then I ran to the post office and told the wrecking ball operator to stop."

The Ghastly Post Office sustained minor damage from a single swing of the wrecking ball. U.S. Postmaster General Sal U. Tayshuns suffered more significant damage. (See story on next page.)

Kids Crash Wrecking Ball

So much for resting in peace.

Late last night Wynonna Fye and Seymour Hope escaped from Greater Ghastly Memorial Hospital. Using a rope and pulley outside the window of room 5, the duo shinnied down the exterior of the building and then raced across town, where they revealed the mystery behind the phantom of the post office.

Dr. Dedyet listens as Seymour and Wy explain their escape route.

It was the first time Hope and Fye had met face to face since they arrived at Greater Ghastly Memorial Hospital last month. They were being treated in separate rooms for phantom flu.

"I suppose this means they're well enough to be released," said Dr. Dedyet. "But I'd like to examine them one last time, just to be sure."

Mr. and Mrs. Fye are scheduled to arrive in Ghastly later today to pick up their daughter. Wy Fye will likely leave town without her favorite digital device.

By texting M. Balm at 11:59 P.M., Miss Fye lost a bet that she could refrain from using a cell phone for the entire month of February.

Post Office Spared, VEXT-mail Shelved and So Long, Sal U. Tayshuns!

It was supposed to be an evening of endings and beginnings. And in a sense, it was.

Plans to replace regular mail service with VEXT-mail have been terminated due to problems with VEXT-mail technology.

"I could've told you VEXT-mail would never fly," said Ghastly Postmaster Sue Perstishus. "Those silly veils never did work right."

On Monday Perstishus will be back at work at the Ghastly Post Office, which will remain open "as long as people believe in letters," said Perstishus.

For decades Perstishus has protected the privacy of all her customers, including former postmaster Weston Peece. "I'm just glad that Mr. Peece was finally able to deliver Olive's acceptance letter." (See story on next page.)

As for Sal U. Tayshuns, the former U.S. postmaster general has been relieved of his

Sue thinks Sal would be happy at Phantom Ranch.

duties and is awaiting reassignment.

"I know the perfect job for Mr. Tayshuns," said Perstishus. "In fact, I've already written a letter to the president of the United States, suggesting that Sal U. Tayshuns be transferred to Phantom Ranch. Can't you just see old Sal delivering mail by mule?"

Here is a copy of the letter Weston Peece delivered to Olive C. Spence.

Dear Olive Christine Spence,

We were most impressed with the manuscripts you sent to us. You are a talented writer and an original storyteller. We hope you will let us publish *all* of your stories in serialized form, as we did with Gaston Leroux's *The Phantom of the Opera*. Please write back as soon as practical and let us know if you would be interested in working with us. We think you have a wonderful career in front of you in both France *and* America! Sincerely,

Z. Nom de Plume

Z. Nom de Plume
Editor, *Le Gaulois*

P.S. I am sending under separate cover a copy of *The Phantom of the Opera.* We believe you will be just as successful as Gaston Leroux, if not more so.

EXCLUSIVE
The Phantom Interview

After his dramatic late night appearance, Weston Peece returned to the basement of the Ghastly Post Office. But before he did, Peece agreed to answer a few remaining questions.

Q: When did you die?

A: I died the day after Olive died. I always thought it was from guilt, but now I know it was likely influenza.

Q: What inspired you to become a phantom rather than a ghost?

A: I got the idea when I read *The Phantom of the Opera*. It arrived the day after Olive's acceptance letter.

Q: You don't mean you read Olive's mail, do you?

A: I did. That's another reason I was too ashamed to show my face.

Q: Did you take the letter "f" hostage?

A: Yes. We phantoms have a lot of tricks up our sleeves. But I simply wanted to make the point that every letter counts.

Q: What about the phantom flu? Was that also one of your tricks?

The phantom responds to lingering questions.

A: It was, and I apologize. But I wanted to help Wy Fye and Seymour Hope become pen pals. I'm so sorry I had to give them both fevers. But honestly, it was nothing worse than the elevated temperatures Olive and I used to get when we read together in front of the fire.

Q: So when Olive said she had fallen under the spell of the post office, she was describing yet another trick of yours, right?

A: Oh, no. A real spell is cast whenever someone sends or receives an old-fashioned letter. It's a spell that can woo or wound, heal or hurt. It's a spell far stronger than any I can cast.

43 Old Cemetery Road
Third Floor
Ghastly, Illinois

March 1

HAND-DELIVERED

Wy Fye
c/o Ghastly Public Library
12 Scary Street
Ghastly, Illinois

Dear Wy,

How can I ever thank you for saving all of our lives last night? I'm just sorry you had to use your cell phone to do it. I know how much you were looking forward to getting it back. But does this mean maybe you'll write to me when you get home? I sure hope so.

You made having the phantom flu fun.

Your friend,

—Seymour

WYNONNA FYE

HAND-DELIVERED

Seymour Hope
43 Old Cemetery Road
Ghastly, Illinois

Dear Seymour,

Apologize? Don't be ridiculous!

Any kid can have a cell phone. (Well, any kid but <u>you</u>, I mean. LOL.) But how many kids can say they've met a phantom and a ghost, and been involved in a postmortem mystery?

It's weird, but it seems like nothing exciting ever happened in my life until I came to Ghastly. So it's true that I lost a bet with my uncle. But I had a ton of fun and gained a friend in the process.

Your BFF (that means Best Friend Forever),

   WY

P.S. Guess what! Uncle M. just gave me back my phone! He said I earned it. 🙂 But let's keep writing letters, okay? It's fun.

P.P.S. You know what my only regret is? We never finished reading <u>The Phantom of the Opera</u>. 🙁

43 Old Cemetery Road
Third Floor
Ghastly, Illinois

March 1

Wy Fye
c/o Ghastly Public Library
12 Scary Street
Ghastly, Illinois

HAND-DELIVERED

Dear Wy,

We have an appointment with Dr. Dedyet at 2:00 today.
I'll bring the book with me and we can finish reading it
together in the waiting room. ☺

Hey, before you leave Ghastly, I want to ask what your
ambition in life is. What's the one thing you want to do
more than anything else on earth? Think about it and LMK,
okay?

     —Seymour

P.S. I don't care if I don't have a cell phone as long as I
have a FLU. (That means Friend Like You!)

IGNATIUS B. GRUMPLY

A WRITER IN RESIDENCE

March 1

Olive C. Spence
The Cupola
43 Old Cemetery Road
Ghastly, Illinois

Dear Olive,

Well, *that* was quite an evening. Who would've guessed the phantom of the post office was your old friend Weston Peece? Or that he only wanted to return a letter to you—an acceptance letter at that!

You must be thrilled to know that the publisher of Gaston Leroux compared your writing to his. I've been doing a bit of research on Leroux. Of course he's most famous today for his Gothic novel *The Phantom of the Opera.* But did you know he was also a pioneer of the detective novel? His heroes used reason and logic to solve mysteries. Sound like anyone we know? Seymour, perhaps? Olive, are you there?

Yes, I'm here.

Aha! So you've abandoned your anti-letter-writing campaign.

Of course I have. But . . . ugh.

Is something wrong?

I've been thinking. Seymour desperately wants a telephone.

It would be nice to have one, Olive. For emergencies, if nothing else.

I just bristle at all these modern contraptions. Technology makes me cranky.

We could get the simplest cell phone. Seymour could teach us how to use it.

Maybe. Oh, good heavens! I just remembered the most marvelous thing! Shortly before my death, I ordered a *brand-new* telephone. It had just been invented. It was supposed to arrive by mail.

And?

I never received it. I wonder if Weston knows where it is. I must ask him. I've started a letter to him.

Olive, is . . . um . . . are you and Weston . . . how shall I put this?

If you're asking whether Weston and I were betrothed, the answer is no.

You seem awfully fond of him.

3

Of course I'm fond of him! We were friends from the time we were seven years old. That was 1825.

I was just wondering if maybe the two of you wanted to pick things up where you left off. Or maybe . . . Oh, Olive, I'm terribly clumsy at these things. But if you want Seymour and me to move out, we will.

Move out? You'll do nothing of the kind. I love you, Iggy. You must know that by now. You and Seymour are my life—or, technically speaking, my *after*life. But old friends are different. You can't make an old friend. You have to keep and treasure the ones you have.

I think I understand.

I knew you would. Besides, there's plenty of room in this mansion for all of us, Weston included. Now go take a nap, dear. You look a bit feverish. I'll deliver your dinner on a tray after I finish my letter to Weston.

O.C.S.

Ghost Writer in Residence
43 Old Cemetery Road, The Cupola
Ghastly, Illinois

March 1

Weston Peece
P.O. Box 5
Ghastly, Illinois

Dear Weston,

I can't tell you how thrilled I am to have rekindled
our friendship. It saddens me to think you've been
hiding from me all these years, ashamed to show
your handsome face.

But enough talk about the past. I'd like to get you
moved into Spence Mansion as soon as possible. As
you know, I have the biggest house in town. Even the
smallest bedroom would be an improvement over the
post office basement. Seymour would love to have
you on the third floor with him. He's such a darling
boy. I know that you two will become friends.

Speaking of Seymour, do you by any chance have the
telephone I ordered in 1911? I have no use for it,

127.

but my family seems to think it's important we own one. Isn't it funny the things we think are important when we're alive? Only in death have I realized the things that really matter to me, and they're not things at all. They're family and friends. Oh, Weston, how could I have died feeling like a failure when I had a friend like you?

I'm so pleased we're writing letters again. Why did you wait so long to get in touch with me?

Love eternally,

Olive

WESTON PEECE
P.O. BOX 5
GHASTLY, ILLINOIS

MARCH 2

OLIVE C. SPENCE
THE CUPOLA
43 OLD CEMETERY ROAD
GHASTLY, ILLINOIS

DEAREST OLIVE,

THANK YOU FOR OFFERING ME A ROOM IN
YOUR MANSION. IT MEANS THE WORLD TO
ME. BUT ODDLY ENOUGH, I'VE BECOME
QUITE COMFORTABLE HERE IN THE POST
OFFICE BASEMENT. I PLAN TO STAY HERE
AS LONG AS I CAN.

I WILL EXPLAIN MY DECISION TO SEYMOUR.
I'M SURE HE'LL UNDERSTAND. HE'S A
SMART BOY, OLIVE. HE ALONE FIGURED
OUT THAT I WASN'T CRYING "I LOVE
CHRISTINE" BUT "OLIVE CHRISTINE."

YOU ASK WHY I WAITED SO LONG TO GET
IN TOUCH WITH YOU. THE TRUTH IS, I
NEVER WOULD HAVE SENT THOSE FAN LET-
TERS IF I HADN'T HEARD THE POST OFFICE
WAS IN DANGER OF CLOSING. I KNOW HOW
MUCH YOU ENJOY WRITING AND RECEIVING
LETTERS, AND HOW IMPORTANT THE POST
OFFICE IS TO THE WORLDWIDE SUCCESS

129.

OF <u>43 OLD CEMETERY ROAD</u>. IN THE END I
DECIDED IT WAS WORTH COMING FORWARD TO
TRY TO SAVE SOMETHING YOU CARE ABOUT SO
DEEPLY. I'M HAPPY IT ALL WORKED OUT.

I'M ALSO HAPPY TO TELL YOU THAT I
HAVE YOUR TELEPHONE. IT'S STILL IN THE
ORIGINAL BOX. I WILL DELIVER IT MYSELF
LATER TODAY.

YOURS TRULY,

WESTON

P.S. YOU KNOW, OLIVE, I ALWAYS WAS YOUR
BIGGEST FAN. AS THE KIDS SAY, THANKS
FOR BEING MY BFF.

And that's how this story ends—
with the residents of
43 Old Cemetery Road
back at home.

They now
have a
phone,
though
it's a bit
old-
fashioned.

They have several
flat screens . . .

. . . though you can't play
video games on them.

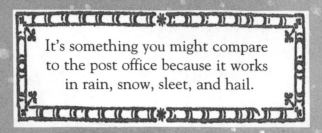

It's something you might compare
to the post office because it works
in rain, snow, sleet, and hail.

What is it?

Love.

Oh, Olive. That's so corny and old-fashioned.

I know, dear. But love is the basis of every friendship and the theme of every great letter. And I
wanted this story to be about friendship and letters,
remember?

I remember. I think it's the perfect ending, Olive.

Thank you, Iggy. Now who would like to read to me
tonight?

I would.

I would.

I WOULD.

Ah, lovely! My first-class males. We shall take
turns reading in front of the fire. Let me just make
a cup of tea. I'll meet you in the parlor posthaste.

The End

for now

(REST IN PEACE.)

Acknowledgments

The author and illustrator would like
to thank our friends
at the U.S. Postal Service,
who for decades have helped us
through rain, snow, sleet, and hail
stay in touch with each other
and with all of our friends
around the world
who share our love of letters
and the written word.

COMING SOON!

Hollywood, Dead Ahead
43 Old Cemetery Road: Book Five

What happens when the ghost of Ghastly meets Hollywood's *femme fatale*?

Lights, camera, action! In this fifth volume from 43 Old Cemetery Road, the creators of everyone's favorite ghost story get an exciting offer in the mail—from Hollywood!

Lured by the lights of Tinseltown and the promise that their story will be a sure-fire hit, Ignatius Grumply, Olive C. Spence, and Seymour Hope pack their suitcases. But when they arrive in Hollywood, Olive has a sure-fire *fit* when she discovers how quickly fame changes Ignatius and Seymour. Olive also discovers that the studio has written her out of the story. "Little old lady ghosts are so yesterday," says producer Moe Block Busters. "What America wants now is a terrifying ghost named Evilo." (That's Olive spelled backwards.)

Well . . . if it's Evilo they want, it's Evilo they'll get. Luckily Olive knows just the person who can help her scare Hollywood's most despicable director half to death.

Told through letters, newspapers, a tell-all tabloid, and a ghostwritten script, *Hollywood, Dead Ahead* is an outrageous romp through the hills and hairpieces of Hollywood.

Rated G for Ghastly-rrific!